Fire Scorcher

Fire Scorcher

Josh Zimmer

CONTENTS

The book is dedicated to writers spending time and effort to write their books with original characters and universes.

The Darkness Returns

In Zoomopolis, there is a technology corporation named Electric Industries, where technology is developed, and several scientists work on experiments for their employees to test. Harry is in his lab, working on various experiments that are stored in tubes. One of these tubes is the alien symbiote that affected and tortured Supersonic Warrior in the past. The alien symbiote caused chaos in Zoomopolis during their previous rampage. The previous rampage caused despair for multiple citizens and caused one of the heroes to kill Supersonic Warrior to protect the city. The symbiote survived the experience though, because one of the Electric Industries employees stored it in the container, before it got destroyed.

The alien symbiote crawled to the side of the container, while Harry was working on his computer. The alien symbiote said, "Free us, we want to bond to our next host, and cause chaos in the city." Harry said, "Not yet, we have to wait for the host to come to us." The alien symbiote sighs, as the prison guards open the door. The prison guards had Powersurge handcuffed, as they walked in to Harry's lab. The prison guards said that Powersurge was recently defeated by Fire Scorcher, and Harry needs to approve him for entry in to the prison, and analyze his physical health before he is accepted to have an prison cell. Powersurge growled, as he struggled in the handcuffs. Harry said, "Don't worry, Powersurge, I won't hurt you, once your tests are finished, you can head to your prison cell or help me with an small task, it's your choice." Powersurge nodded and said, "Fine, I want revenge on Fire Scorcher for defeating me." Harry nodded and said, "Don't worry, depending on my task for you, you might get to have some fun with our little hero, Fire Scorcher, with the experiment that I am working on". Powersurge was interested in the offer. Harry said, "The experiment will enhance your strength and power, this will help you defeat Fire Scorcher, if he doesn't outsmart you. Powersurge nodded as Harry took off the handcuffs. Harry shook Powersurge's hand, as they smirked.

Powersurge laid in the experiment tube, as Harry connected the wires to his body. Harry pressed the buttons on the computer, Harry said, "You will feel an small tingle, and don't worry, the alien symbiote is immune to electricity, so your powers won't fry it when attached to your body." Powersurge nodded, as Harry pressed the button, and the alien symbiote covered Powersurge's body. Powersurge's armor turned black as the symbiote enhanced his powers.The experiment was an success, as Harry smirked. Harry disconnected Powersurge from the tube, as he climbed out of it. Powersurge felt powerful and enhanced, as he used his electricity and symbiote tendrils to destroy the practice containers on the ground. Harry was pleased with his work, as he shook Powersurge's hand. Powersurge powered himself up with his electric symbiote aura, as he climbed out of the window. Powersurge flew through the city to look for Fire Scorcher. Powersurge landed at the gas station, and used his symbiote tendrils to destroy it, as he caused chaos in the city with the gas station exploding.Further down the street, Deku and Shoto saw the chaos on the television. Shoto said, "It is Sparky Mc Spark Spark again, looks like the security team failed to transport him to the prison." Shoto pressed the button on his wrist and transformed in to Fire Scorcher, as he kissed Deku's forehead for support. Deku went to his room, as Fire Scorcher flew toward Powersurge's location. Fire Scorcher saw Powesurge and kicked him in the face. Powersurge smirked, as he brabbed Fire Scorcher's leg and slammed him in to the pole with an lightning blast to the chest.

Fire Scorcher backflipped and laned on the ground. Powersurge said, "The hero is here to lecture me about my emotions again, how cute." Powersurge blasted Fire Scorcher in the chest multiple times, as he get blasted through multiple walls while they crumble. Powersurge said, "I don't need your emotional lectures, I got an power upgrade, and I am not afraid to hurt you and everyone else to get what I want." Powersurge used his electrical superspeed to blast and punch Fire Scorcher from all sides before Fire Scorcher could react. Fire Scorcher tried to scan his surroundings but Powersurge moved quickly, and blasted him in the face with an powerful electrical blast. The electrical blast smashed him through an 20 foot glass skyscraper, as it shattered while Fire Scorcher rolled on the ground, and smashed through an car windshield as it shattered and dented. Powersurge used his electrical symbiote tendrils to smash Fire Scorcher through the street as the cars exploded, causing Fire Scorcher to lay in an crater to catch his breath. Fire Scorcher got up and rubbed his head as Powersurge growled and laned in front of him with an black electrical symbiotic aura. Fire Scorcher said, " You feel and act differently than the previous fights. Powersurge said, "It's part of my power upgrade, thanks to my friend at Electric Industries. You probably heard of them, they are the biggest technological corporation in Zoomopolis."

Fire Scorcher said, "I beat you twice, I can beat you again, regardless of your upgrades." Powersurge said, "Typical hero logic, being overconfident in your skills." Powersurge used his electric symbiotic tendrils to smash Fire Scorcher in to the wall. Fire Scorcher growled, and blasted Powersurge in the chest with his fire blast. Powersurge said, "My upgrade added resistance to fire." Powersurge used his speed to grab Fire Scorcher's head and blasted his body with electricity. Fire Scorcher winced in pain, as he bent down on the ground, from the pain. Powersurge kicked Fire Scorcher in to the pole, as he laid next to it. Powersurge attached multiple symbiotic tendrils to Fire Scorcher, as he was attached to the pole. Powersurge smirked, as he used his electricity on the pole to electrocute Fire Scorcher at full blast. The electricity flowed through Fire Scorcher's body, as he got electrocuted. Powersurge laughed as he used the symbiote tendrils to beat up Fire Scorcher while he got electrocuted. Fire Scorcher screamed in pain, as the symbiote tendrils slashed through his suit, causing deep wounds on his body. Fire Scorcher's suit was being burnt from the electricity and torn to shreds from the tendrils, as he laid on the ground, with heavy breathing from the deep wounds on his body.

Powersurge said, "Look how the mighty has fallen, my new and improved powers defeated the hero, and now the city will suffer, thanks to you." Powersurge ignited an electric explosion from his body, causing every building to crumble around him, with thousands of citizens dying. Fire Scorcher laid on the ground, and tried to get up, as he heard thousands of citizens dying and laying on the ground in puddles of blood around him. Fire Scorcher said, "No, what have you done?" Powersurge said, "I have no remorse as an free soul." Powersurge used an symbiote tendril to stab Fire Scorcher in the back. Fire Scorcher laid on the ground, as Powersurge smashed Fire Scorcher in to an crater with the symbiote tendrils. Fire Scorcher laid on the ground, barely conscious, as his suit repaired his wounds and his body. Powersurge smirked, as he flew in to the air, to scout for Deku. Fire Scorcher shouted, "Don't hurt him, Deku is my friend."

Fire Scorcher's body healed, as his breathing returned to normal. Fire Scorcher flew after Powersurge, back to Deku's location. Powersurge spotted Deku's house on the radar as he landed. Fire Scorcher landed at Deku's house, as he scouted the area for Powersurge. The deep wounds from Fire Scorcher's body haven't healed yet, as he was wincing in pain from scouting the area. He saw Powersurge walk in to Deku's house, as he slowly walked in, to stay out of Powersurge's range. Fire Scorcher went in to Deku's room, and was relived that Deku was safe. Powersurge walked in to Deku's room, as Fire Scorcher tackled Powersurge to the ground. Fire Scorcher pinned Powersurge to the ground, as he blasted him with Sonic blasts. Powersurge winced in pain, as the sonic blasts were hurting the symbiote. Powersurge said, "Nooooo, it hurts so much, the symbiote is angry." Deku caused another sonic blast by hitting Powersurge in the chest. Fire Scorcher and Deku were blasting Powersurge with sonic blasts, as he rolled and screamed in pain, from the sonic blasts hurting the symbiote. Powersurge screamed in pain, as his electric aura and eyes started to glow. Powersurge said, "Leave my symbiote alone, he makes me stronger. Powersurge ignited an electric explosion, as the area covered in electricity, while electrocuting Deku and Fire Scorcher. Deku and Fire Scorcher hugged Powersurge, as his emotions took over Powersurge's blasts. After multiple hours, Powersuge cooled down, as his emotions exploded in to tears, while Fire Scorcher and Deku hugged him. Powersurge's symbiote was fried from the sonic blasts, Fire Scorcher and Deku put the symbiote in to the container as Powersurge laid on the ground. Powersurge said, "I need the symbiote, it's the only thing that I have left for power after losing my brother, I don't want to lose the symbiote." Fire Scorcher said, "I know you have a grudge against me. Power and strength isn't the answer for revenge." Powersurge said, "Don't lecture me, I won't listen to you." Fire Scorcher sighed and led Powersurge to the spare bedroom. Fire Scorcher said, "You need to rest, you must be exhausted from your power blasts, you need to be energized for your employer." Powersurge nodded, as he powered down, and fell asleep under the bed sheets. Deku and Fire Scorcher sighed as they laid on the couch, cuddling. Fire Scorcher powered down with the button on his wrist. Deku and Shoto smiled, as they cuddled on the couch together. Shoto said, "Today was rough." Deku nodded and said, "Don't worry, I will make your day better." Shoto and Deku smiled at each other as they cuddled for comfort.

Several hours have passed while Deku and Shoto cuddled and slept together until the morning sun rose in the sky. Shoto woke up before Deku, as Shoto stretched and got up from the couch. Shoto laid the blanket over Deku, as he noticed Powersurge outside by himself. Shoto was cautious as he walked closer to Powersurge. Shoto leaned against the wall, as he saw Powersurge talking to the alien symbiote that was attached to him.The alien symbiote said, "Harry let me attach to you, because you were strong and powerful. You're disappointing us." Powersurge said, "I am sorry, give me another chance." The alien symbiote said, "You wanted revenge on Fire Scorcher, and you have failed to fulfill your promise to us. You had Fire Scorcher on the chopping block, and laying on the ground, until he outsmarted you." Powersurge said, "I will do better next time." The alien symbiote said, "Prove to us thaat you are useful, or we will force ourselves to detach from you, and find an new host, that is better for our entertainment." Powersurge said, "I promise!" The alien symbiote said, "Don't disappoint us." Powersurge smirked, as he saw Fire Scorcher leaning against the wall.

Powersurge said, "Ready for another round of pain, I need to prove to my little friend that I am using the full potential of my powers" Fire Scorcher nodded, as he got in to his fighting stance.Fire Scorcher used his speed to outsmart Powersurge as he ran around him, and pummeled him with punches to all sides of his body. Powersurge analyzed the movement of Fire Scorcher and blocked all of the attacks with his symbiote tendrils. Fire Scorcher was shocked that Powersurge blocked the attacks. Powersurge smirked, and blasted Fire Scorcher through the tree with his symbiote tendrils. Fire Scorcher rolled on the ground and backflipped in to position. Powersurge charged toward Fire Scorcher, as Fire Scorcher jumped over him, and kicked him in the back. Powersurge stumbled as he shot an electric blast at Fire Scorcher. Fire Scorcher dodged and kicked Powersurge in the face. Powersurge grabbed Fire Scorcher's leg, and slammed him in to the ground multiple times. Fire Scorcher growled, as Powersurge blasted Fire Scorcher in the chest, smashing through the treehouse as it crumbled on to the ground. Fire Scorcher breathed heavily, as he bent down on his hands and knees, to catch his breath, while the treehouse crumbled around him.

Powersurge smirked as he punched Fire Scorcher in the face, multiple times as he laid on the ground. Powersurge said, :You're in my grasp now, and I will deal as much pain as possible." Fire Scorcher laid on the ground, handling the pain, as Powersurge pummeled him with punches, kicks, and electric blasts to the body. Fire Scorcher's mask shattered as Powersurge wrapped Fire Scorcher in an cocoon with his symbiote tendrils and smashed him in to the ground and everything around him multiple times. Fire Scorcher laid on the ground, as Powersurge electrified himself with an electric symbiotic blast, that smashed him and Fire Scorcher through multiple buildings as there were explosions around them. Powersurge and Fire Scorcher breathed heavily as they laid on the ground. Fire Scorcher slowly got up and noticed that the explosion detached the symbiote from Powersurge as he saw the symbiote surging next to Powersurge. Powersurge said, "Symbiote, don't leave me." The alien symbiote said, "You're too strong, our strength conflicts with each other." Powersurge said, " Noooooooooo, come back." The alien symbiote growled as it crawled away, moving closer to Fire Scorcher." The alien symbiote said, "Fire Scorcher looks like an delicious host to devor and love." Powersurge broke down and cried, "Nooooooooooo, I lost my brother, and now I am losing the symbiote that Harry gave me." Powersurge bent down on his knees and cried as tears poured from his eyes. The alien symbiote crawls on to Fire Scorcher and took over his body in a cocoon of symbiote tendrils. The alien symbiote said, "You're so delicious and powerful, we would make good friends, if you don't stab us in the back." Fire Scorcher growled and nodded, as the alien symbiote covered his suit with black symbiotic armor, as he obtained an black symbiotic aura, and glowing black eyes. Fire Scorcher growled, as he walked closer to Powersurge. Powersurge said, "You took the alien symbiote away from me, give him back." Powersurge growled, as he punched Fire Scorcher in the chest. Fire Scorcher grabbed Powersurge's arm, and smashed him in to the wall with an symbiote tendril. Fire Scorcher hit Powersurge in the chest and pummeled him with multiple symbiote tendrils as he smashed through the wall. Fire Scorcher used his symbiote speed to pummel Powersurge as he smashed him in to the ground with an powerful force. Fire Scorcher used his symbiote grip to smash Powersurge through the ground, as Powersurge growled.

Powersurge used his electricity to backflip and kick Fire Scorcher in the face. Fire Scorcher barely finched and kicked him in to the pole, as it fell over. Powersurge growled, as he grabbed the pole, and hit Fire Scorcher in the chest with it. Fire Scorcher backflipped over the pole, and smashed Powersurge's head in to the car windshield. Powersurge kicked Fire Scorcher backwards as he backflipped off of the car hood. Fire Scorcher wrapped Powersurge in an cocoon of symbiotic tendrils. Powersurge ignited his body, as the tendrils melted. Harry flew over the area, and saw that the alien symbiote left Powersurge and attached itself to the hero. Harry growled, as he used his glider to paralyze Powersurge. Powersurge got paralyzed by the glider missile, as he froze in place. Powersurge said, "I can't move, the paralysis is shutting down my body. Fire Scorcher smirked, as he used the symbiote tentrills to smash Powersurge in to the wall. Powersurge laid on the ground, barely conscious. Harry landed his glider in front of Fire Scorcher, as he laid Powersurge on his back. Harry said, "I am taking Powersurge back to my lab for further tests. Thanks for entertaining my little experiment." Fire Scorcher nodded as he growled at Harry. Harry smirked as he flew out of the area with Powersurge, back to his lab.

Harry shot a missile at Katsuki, and the missile contained lizard dna from one of his recent experiments. The lizard dna went in to Katsuki's body, and turned him into an lizard. Katsuki growled in his lizard form, and tackled Fire Scorcher through multiple buildings. Katsuki clawed through Fire Scorcher's body, as they smashed through multiple buildings. Fire Scorcher growled as Katsuki slammed through multiple buildings and streets killing civilians in their path. Katsuki threw Fire Scorcher in to the bridge, as Fire Scorcher stumbled, and regained his footing. Katsuki smashed the Fire Scorcher in to the car with his tail. Fire Scorcher was having trouble analyzing Katsuki's movements. Fire Scorcher used his symbiote tendrils to attack Katsuki, but Katsuki dodged each attack. Katsuki knocked Fire Scorcher in to the water with his tail. Fire Scorcher landed in the water, as Katsuki dived after him. Katsuki and Fire Scorcher were underwater as they tackled and attacked each other. The symbiote gave Fire Scorcher the ability to breathe underwater as Katsuki punched Fire Scorcher in the chest with his claws. Fire Scorcher grabbed Katsuki's tail, and slammed him in to an rock. Katsuki growled, as Fire Scorcher grabbed Katsuki's tail, and threw him out of the water. Fire Scorcher used his symbiotic powers to launch out of the water, as he slammed Katsuki through multiple mountains at superspeed without stopping with punches and kicks at supersonic speed. They smashed through a snowy mountain as they rolled on the beach. Katsuki and Fire Scorcher regained their footing as they took their stances.

Katsuki charged towards Fire Scorcher and grabbed his neck to pin him to the ground. Katsuki scratched Fire Scorcher's chest and pierced through the armor, stabbing Fire Scorcher in the chest with an deep wound. Fire Scorcher growled as the symbiote made him stronger with his emotions. Fire Scorcher shot an tendril from his chest in to Katsuki's neck, and pushed himself upward with the tendrils, as more symbiote tendrils stabbed in to Katsuki's body. The symbiote used its draining powers to immoblize Katsuki and drain the lizard blood out of him. Katsuki laid on the ground with the symbiote aura glowing around Fire Scorcher. Fire Scorcher growled, with his fanged teeth sharpening, as he walked closer to Katsuki. Katsuki was terrified and moved back, while Fire Scorcher got closer. Katsuki said, "Don't hurt me, I am just an normal citizen, just like you.

Fire Scorcher said, "We won't hurt you, we want to devour you and absorb your soul. Katsuki said, "Noooooo, this isn't like you, heroes don't hurt people." Fire Scorcher said, "we aren't your normal hero, we are powerful and invincible." Fire Scorcher doesn't notice that Deku tracked him on the GPS to his current location, and was hiding behind an tree. Fire Scorcher growled, and grabbed Katsuki in an tight grip." Katsuki said, "Don't hurt me." Fire Scorcher tighten his grip on Katsuki's neck. Katsuki said while struggling to breathe," Let go of me, this isn't you at all, the alien symbiote has took over your mind and soul." Fire Scorcher said, "We are in control of our emotions and you must die." Fire Scorcher shot symbiote tendrils to smush and crush Katsuki's body. Katsuki said, "Aaugh, stop, you're hurting me." Fire Scorcher smirked and said, "Good." Fire Scorcher shot an symbiote tendril in to Katsuki's chest." The symbiote tendril stabbed Katsuki and killed him in an puddle of blood. Deku was horrified when he saw what happened behind the tree. Deku picked up an rock and threw it at Fire Scorcher. Fire Scorcher dodged and walked closer to Deku's location. Deku said, "Don't come any closer, if I were you."

Fire Scorcher said, "Deku, I won't hurt you." Deku stepped back and said, "I have seen you kill Katsuki and badly injure Powersurge, the alien symbiote is turning you in to an monster, and I am scared that you're going to hurt me as well with the alien symbiote. Fire Scorcher said, "I am not an monster, and I won't hurt you." Deku stepped back, as Fire Scorcher got closer to him. Fire Scorcher pressed the button on his wrist and turned off his suit. Shoto slowly walked to Deku. Deku was hesitant to walk closer to Shoto. Deku hid behind an tree, as Shoto walked closer. Deku saw that Shoto was next to him. Deku punched Shoto in the face and pushed him to the ground. Shoto was shocked that Deku punched him, since they cuddled with each other in the past. Shoto rubbed his face, where Deku punched him. Deku said, "You have an alien symbiote attached to you, get rid of it, or I will force you to get rid of it." Shoto growled, as the alien symbiote used its tendrils to help Shoto off the ground. Deku said, "Make one move, and I am going to hurt you until that evil symbiote leaves your body." Shoto walked closer, as he growled. Deku said, "I am warning you, if you attack me, I won't give you an chance to hurt me." Shoto growled, ashe shot symbiote tendrils at Deku. Deku dodged and shot sonic blasts at Shoto. The sonic blasts hit Shoto as the alien symbiote screamed in pain. Deku continued to shoot Shoto with sonic blasts as Shoto laid against the wall with the alien symbiote screaming in pain. Shoto growled and said, "Stop shooting me, or I will do something that I am going to regret." Deku growled and said, "Give me my friend back, alien symbiote." Deku continued to blast Shoto as the symbiote tendrils shot out of Shoto's body, pulling Deku closer to Shoto. Deku shot the symbiote tendrils with sonic blasts to try to weaken the grip of them. The alien symbiote growled, as it shot a tendril out of Shoto's body and destroyed the sonic blast gun in Deku's hand. Deku stumbled back, as Shoto leaned against the wall. Deku's eyes darken with anger as he dodged every tendril. Deku kicked Shoto in the face as he stumbled backwards. Shoto and the symbiote growled as it smashed Deku through the car as it exploded with an tendril. Deku smashed in to the wall, as the symbiote attacked Deku with more tendrils. Deku grabbed the tendril and threw Shoto in to the gas station pump, causing the gas station and the other pumps to explode. The explosion smashed Shoto in to an power tower, as it electrocuted him and the symbiote. Shoto and the symbiote growled, as his body smoked from the electrocution.. Shoto got up from the ground and growled, as he charged toward Deku. Deku dodged and hit Shoto in the back with an metal bat. Shoto growled in pain, as he slammed in to the pole, knocking it over. Shoto said, "Deku, why are you hurting me." Deku said, "You're affected with the alien symbiote, it's making you act like an villain. Shoto said, "I am sorry, but I don't want to hurt you. Deku said, "I know, but you're not yourself with the evil ooze." Shoto growled as alien symbiote tendrils shot out of his body, and smashed Deku in to the wall. Shoto said, "We are in control, surrender or be destroyed." Deku growled and said, "Shoto, this isn't you, stop now." Shoto said, "Never!" Deku used the metal pole, trapping Shoto in an sound cage, as he whacked it as hard as he could. The sound vibrations were making Shoto and the symbiote growl in pain. Deku continues to hit the metal poles to make sound blasts to hurt Shoto and the alien symbiote. The alien symbiote growled in pain, as it got angrier to try to stop the vibrations. Shoto grabbed Deku with multiple tendrils, crushing him in to the ground. Deku struggled and said, "Stop, you're hurting me" The tendrils crushed Deku's body as he got pushed further in to the ground." Shoto growled as his eyes were black with anger.

Deku hesitated, as he was in a tricky situation. Deku pressed an button on his wrist and punched Shoto in the chest with his sonic gauntlet, which smashed Shoto through the building. Deku backflipped out of the crater and pinned Shoto to the ground with an arm lock. Deku tightened his grip on Shoto's neck. Shoto struggled as he was pinned to the ground. Deku punched Shoto in the chest with his arm with multiple sonic and electric blasts to weaken the symbiote and Shoto. Shoto was getting weaker, as his eyes returned to normal. The electric blasts paralyzed the symbiote and temporarily weakened it. Deku sighed in relief, as Shoto collapsed on the ground from exhaustion. Deku laid Shoto on his back, and rode his skateboard back to his house. Deku walked in to his first aid room, that was in his house. Deku opened his medical tube and attached Shoto to the wires. Deku started up the healing tube, as it detached the symbiote from Shoto's body, and put the symbiote in to an separate tube. Shoto's body started to heal and patch up all of the injuries and wounds on his body from the exhausting battle that he went through. Deku continued to monitor Shoto's condition,

Further down the street, Harry transported Powersurge back to Electric Industries for further experiments. Harry plugged Powersurge in to the chair, as he connected the wires to Powersurge's body and strapped him to the chair. Powersurge said, "Let me go, I am not done torturing Fire Scorcher for revenge. Harry said, "You have failed my expectations, you're not ready to fight against Fire Scorcher again, until your body gets upgraded. Powersurge said, "Fire Scorcher made me kill my brother and caused me pain and suffering, I want to kill him and get revenge on him." Harry said, "The pain and suffering that you went through was from your own actions. Your actions killed your brother and everyone in the city." Fire Scorcher didn't force you to kill them, your emotions channeled your actions to cause chaos around you." Powersurge said, "I didn't sign up for your life lessons, scientist." Harry said, "I am just telling you the truth, the truth strikes you down hard, like a powerful punch from your mortal enemy." Harry pressed the buttons, and the wires electrocuted Powersurge with electrical energy to power himself up with." Powersurge screamed in anger as he channeled the electricity.. Harry smirked, "I hope that powered you up, because that was only step one of your upgrades. Powersurge smiled as Harry continued to experiment with him. Harry said, "Once i'm done, Fire Scorcher won't know what he's dealing with during your next fight.